D1046191

All Wrapped Up

Written by Thera S. Callahan

Illustrated by Mike Gordon

Children's Press®
A Division of Scholastic Inc.
New York • Toronto • London • Auckland • Sydney
Mexico City • New Delhi • Hong Kong
Danbury, Connecticut

For Katie and Claire
—T.S.C.

Reading Consultants

Linda Cornwell
Literacy Specialist

Katharine A. Kane
Education Consultant
(Retired, San Diego County Office of Education and San Diego State University)

Library of Congress Cataloging-in-Publication Data
Callahan, Thera S.
  All wrapped up / written by Thera S. Callahan ; illustrated by Mike
Gordon.– 1st American ed.
     p. cm. – (Rookie reader)
Summary: When a brother and sister run out of tape while tryng to wrap
their dad's birthday present, they use various other sticky substances
to make the paper stick.
  ISBN 0-516-22844-7 (lib. bdg.)   0-516-21949-9 (pbk.)
  [1. Gifts–Fiction. 2. Brothers and sisters–Fiction. 3. Humorous
stories.] I. Gordon, Mike, ill. II. Title. III. Series.
  PZ7.C12945AI 2003
  [E]–dc21
                              2003003780

It is Dad's birthday.

We have his gift,
but there is no tape.

We could use
gummy glue sticks,

or fluffy frosting,

or baby bandages,

10

11

or slippery syrup,

or gooey gum,

or mushy marshmallows,

or runny honey,

or sticky stamps,

21

or tacky taffy,

or jiggly jelly.

What would work best?
We did not know.

So we used a little of this and a little of that.

And the paper stuck.

Word List (57 words)

a	his	sticks
all	honey	sticky
and	is	stuck
baby	it	syrup
bandages	jelly	tacky
best	jiggly	taffy
birthday	know	tape
but	little	that
could	marshmallows	the
Dad's	mushy	there
did	no	this
fluffy	not	up
frosting	of	use
gift	or	used
glue	paper	we
gooey	runny	what
gum	slippery	work
gummy	so	would
have	stamps	wrapped

About the Author
Thera S. Callahan lives with her family in Philadelphia, Pennsylvania. Her daughters, Katie and Claire, love doing arts and crafts and often use a lot of tape. Sometimes they run out. Their adventures in finding alternative sticky substances was the inspiration for this book. Thera has also written *Sara Joins the Circus* in the *A Rookie Reader* series.

About the Illustrator
Mike Gordon lives in sunny Santa Barbara, California, where he spends his days illustrating humorous books, greeting cards, and eating chocolate chip cookies with his two kids, Kim and Jay. Carl Gordon lives in England and worked on a computer to add the color to Mike's pictures for this book.